1995

Given to the
Veterans' Memorial
School Library
in honor of
Robert Penta

© 1987 GAYLORD

Good Griselle

Good Griselle

AN ORIGINAL TALE BY

JANE YOLEN

ILLUSTRATED BY

DAVID CHRISTIANA

HARCOURT BRACE & COMPANY

SAN DIEGO · NEW YORK · LONDON

Requests for permission to make copies of any part of the work
should be mailed to: Permissions Department,
Harcourt Brace & Company, 6277 Sea Harbor Drive,
Orlando, Florida 32887-6777.

Library of Congress Cataloging-in-Publication Data
Yolen, Jane.
Good Griselle/written by Jane Yolen; illustrated by
David Christiana. — 1st ed.
p. cm.
Summary: Angels and gargoyles test a woman's goodness by providing
her with an ugly baby to love.
ISBN 0-15-231701-5
[1. Angels — Fiction. 2. Babies — Fiction.] I. Christiana, David,
ill. II. Title.
PZ7.Y78Go   1994
[Fic] — dc20   93-11691
First edition
A B C D E
Printed in Singapore

3/95 The Bookstore 14.95

For Ann and Joel and David
and our weekend in Paris, 1989 — J. Y.

To my loving and patient
wife, Kristie — D. C.

I N OLD PARIS, not far from a great cathedral, lived a lace maker whose name was Griselle.

When she was young, Griselle had been very beautiful and many men had courted her. There had been a barrel maker, a cheese merchant, a burly blacksmith, a shy scholar. Once the baron himself, when he came to worship at the cathedral, had thrown her a rose and asked her name.

But Griselle had married none of them. She chose instead a poor, laughing soldier named Beau, who wore a bright red plume like a flame in his hat.

Alas, before they'd been married a week, Beau and all his regiment were marched off to war. Griselle never saw or heard from him again.

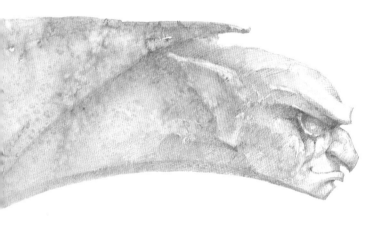

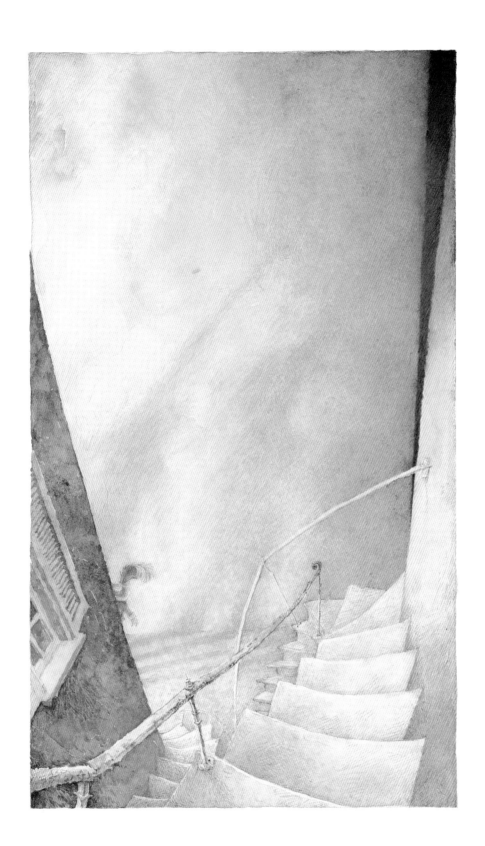

The years went by and Griselle was neither widow nor wife. Yet she did not despair. It was not in her nature to do so. Instead she devoted herself to all the little creatures who lived in the shadow of the cathedral, feeding them from her own meager stores. They became her children.

Every day, rain or sun, wind or calm, Griselle would walk by the cathedral and cross the bridge to market. There she would purchase a loaf of bread and fill her pitcher with fresh milk. Half the loaf and half the milk she kept to herself. But the rest she always gave away, crumbling the bread into tiny bits for the birds and pouring the milk into little bowls, which she set down in the bushes for the cats who lived nearby.

All the birds and cats loved Griselle as if she were their mother. They counted on her coming through rain or sun, through wind or calm. One thrush especially loved her and left the woods at the edge of Paris to sing each evening at her window. And there was an orange tomcat she called Monsieur, who occasionally came into her house to curl up by the hearth and purr as loudly as a man snores.

It was company — of a sort.

Year after year Griselle made her living working miracles of lace, and year after year she gave away half her food. She was in her way quite content.

And then one day the stone angels on the cathedral wall noticed her. They commented about her in that strange, soft whisper that only stone angels use and which passers-by mistake for the cooing of doves.

"See," said one, "here she comes again."

"She never forgets," said a second.

"She never will," added a third.

They sang Griselle's praises until their voices reached the stone gargoyles who squatted precariously on the ledges and edges of the cathedral, spitting out water after every rain.

Now if there is one thing gargoyles cannot stand, having been made in the ugly image of the devil himself, it is the look and smell of a good woman. They hate hearing of it even more than they hate hearing of a good man. Indeed, to hear such a woman praised hurt their ears. So they began to complain together, in that strange, hard grumbling that only stone gargoyles use and which passers-by mistake for the rumbling of carts.

"She is not as good as she seems," said one.

"No one is," said a second.

"We must test her," added a third, scratching himself in unpleasant places, the sound of which was remarkably like chalk scraping on slate.

So late that night, when all of Paris slept beneath them, the gargoyles sent one of their own to speak with the angels, to propose a wager. And because it was Christmas Eve, the angels agreed to listen.

"Anyone," the gargoyle messenger said, his ugly face screwed up into a most disagreeable and permanent sneer, "*anyone* can be good when it comes to the feeding of cats and birds. But we mean to test this Good Griselle with something far more difficult."

The stone angels, whose faces were fixed in permanent holy smiles, inclined their heads slowly to one side, meaning they were willing to listen further. It was, after all, Christmas Eve — and as angels they had been made to be charitable.

"We want to test her with an ugly and unlovable child," the gargoyle said. "Even good mothers come to grief over such."

"She is too old for a child," pointed out the chief angel, looking down her long nose at the gargoyle and wrinkling it slightly, as if she had just smelled something horrible. And surely if stone could smell bad, the gargoyle would have. "Besides," the stone angel continued, having worn out her charity, "her husband is many years gone. She cannot have a child."

The gargoyle almost smiled, which improved neither his disposition nor his looks. *He* had no birthright of charity. "*We* will supply the child," he said in his grumble of a voice, "if *you* promise not to aid Griselle in any way."

The angels all nodded their stone heads at that because they knew interference in such matters could only come from instructions from on high. And the sound of their heads nodding was like the sound of red plumes waving in the breeze. Down below, in her narrow bed, Griselle dreamed of her young husband and how he had looked going off to war. It was a dream that was both happy and sad, and she laughed and wept in her sleep but did not awaken.

"Agreed," cooed the angels, sure of their own success.

"And," the gargoyle added, knowing that once an angel has agreed to a wager, it is impossible for her to back out of the rest, "if we are correct and Griselle is not *really* good, one of you shall join us squatting on a ledge of the cathedral, spitting out rainwater and cursing God's name for one hundred years."

There was a great flutter of consternation among the angels, and the sound of it caused the bells to tremble in the steeple. But remembering Griselle's goodness, all the angels at last agreed.

"However," the chief angel said smugly, knowing that gargoyles, too, must keep to a bargain, "if *we* are correct and she is as good as we say, then one of you shall have to stand upright with us, back straight, singing hosannahs to the heavens for one hundred years."

For a moment the gargoyle looked concerned. His face cracked in several places, causing slivers of stone to rain down on the street below. But remembering at last the imperfection of mankind, he grinned his agreement and the bargain was struck.

And so that very night a strange shape was flung down from the top of the cathedral, twisting and turning as it fell. It landed right by Griselle's door with a horrible thud that scattered birds from their nests and forced Monsieur from his cozy place by the fire, though the cold was bone-chilling outside.

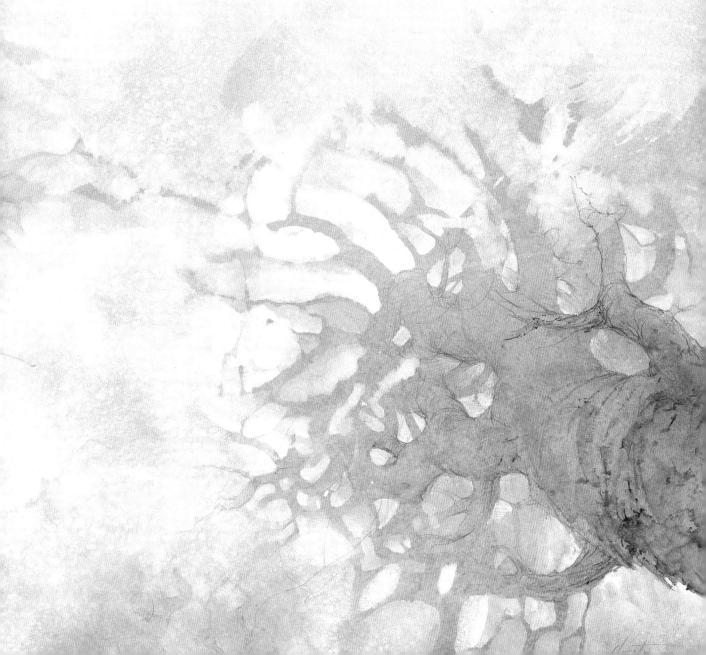

Only Griselle did not awaken at the sound. Indeed, she would have slept the whole night through, dreaming of her young husband, Beau, if the creature at her door had not begun to cry.

It was a pitiful wail—part sob, part laugh—and it went on and on and on, shattering the Christmas peace of Paris.

Griselle arose, holding her old dressing gown closed with one hand. When she opened the door, there in front of her was the ugliest child she had ever seen.

He was so ugly his eyes crossed, and his nose and chin threatened to meet in the middle. His ears stuck out of corn-colored hair like two horns. His teeth were nearly black.

Griselle shuddered. For a moment she thought he was an imp of Satan, and surely that was not a sight for Christmas Day. But when the ugly child cried again, part sob and part laugh, she held the door open further, motioning him in, for she knew the devil did not know how to weep.

The ugly child did not move. Indeed, it was as if his feet were rooted to the ground. But he held up his hands. "Mama!" he cried in a voice as cracked as old leather.

"Poor little thing," Griselle said. She bent down and picked him up, wrinkling her nose slightly at his smell, for he was as ripe as a dish of milk left out too long in the sun. When she straightened with the child in her arms, he was as heavy as a sin. But still she smiled at him.

When the stone angels saw this, they, too, smiled. One even began humming a benison, until the nearest gargoyle called out, "Hush! Tush! You may not help!" in a voice like a cartwheel needing to be oiled. The angel stopped singing.

The ugly little boy grabbed a hank of Griselle's hair and pulled hard. Griselle gave a scream.

When they heard that, the gargoyles sneered. One even started to chortle, until the nearest angel called out, "Hush! Tush! *You* may not help!" in a voice like that of an early lark. The gargoyle stopped laughing.

Griselle cocked her head for a moment, as if she had heard both the song and the laughter. Then she shrugged. *After all, Paris is always full of noise.* And carrying the ugly little boy hard against her breast, she went into the house and closed the door.

Through winter and spring and the hot Paris summer, through rain and sun and wind and calm, Griselle took care of the ugly little boy. She combed his corn-colored hair and wiped his crooked nose and made him clothes out of her own: a white linen shirt from her petticoat, a pair of blue pants from her cloak, and a vest made from her wedding gown, covered with shiny buttons and little pearls. His clothes were handsome, though his face was not, and she called him Beau, after her lost husband, thinking he might grow into the name.

When Beau yanked the cat's tail and stole eggs from the thrush's nest, she cautioned him saying: "A gentle hand is best."

When he overturned the barrel maker's barrels and threw about the cheese maker's wares, she chided: "Do to others as you would be done by."

And when he took coins from the poor box in the cathedral, she made him put them back double. "For others," she reminded him, "are not so fortunate as we."

And if the barrel maker and the cheese maker, the thrush and the cat, the neighbors for blocks around — and even the baron himself — called the ugly little boy Gargoyle, cursing his name, Griselle did not. For she had learned to love him. And when she tucked him into her bed at night, kissing his ugly little face on both cheeks and brow, she thought, *He is company. Am I not lucky to have such?*

So most of the year passed, with little Beau playing one rascally trick after another. But nothing he did made Griselle love him any less.

Up on their ledges, the stone gargoyles grew worried. There was nothing they hated more than losing a wager, and a Christmas wager at that. They grumbled continuously through the fall months, sounding like thunder. All the good folk who lived near the cathedral gazed skyward day after day, expecting rain.

The angels, though, looked smugly complacent. And it was their very smugness that almost proved Griselle's undoing, for they were not listening when the gargoyles prayed to their own dark gods for extra aid two nights before Christmas. The angels, it may be remembered, had agreed not to interfere in any way. But the gargoyles, having been bred in deceit, had made no such promise.

And so that very night, down the street marched a handsome soldier, his red plume a bit bedraggled but still waving in the wind. If his face was the color of stone, it was hidden by the dark. If his ears were spiked like horns, they were covered by his hat. And if his smile went only to the teeth and not the eyes—well, that might have been a trick of the moonlight.

He knocked on Griselle's door.

Cautiously, she opened the door and peered out. Visitors rarely came in the evening, never at night. When she saw the soldier framed in the doorway, she thought she must be asleep and dreaming. But when he took her hand in his, she knew she was awake.

"I am home, wife," he said, stepping inside. His smile seemed more glorious than she remembered.

She ran to get him wine and cake, stopping in front of the glass to comb her hair. Her eyes filled with tears seeing how age had taken her while he was still so handsome, so dashing, so young. If she wondered at it, she assumed travel had treated him well.

When she came back into the room, he was standing over the bed where little Beau lay asleep, thumb in his mouth against the black teeth.

"That bed is mine," the soldier said. "Remove him."

Griselle did not say a word but picked up the sleeping child and gently set him, wrapped in a blanket, onto the hearth, where he slept until morn.

At breakfast, when Griselle went to feed little Beau, the soldier complained. "I will not have a child eat what is rightfully mine. Give me his food."

Griselle almost spoke out then, but glancing at the soldier's handsome face, she kept still, taking the food from little Beau's plate and handing it to the man. But secretly, while he was eating it all, she took food from her own meager plate and gave it to the child.

By evening, when the boy had overturned the barrel maker's shop once again and pulled Monsieur's tail, and even plucked the barbs one at a time from the soldier's feathery plume — and that was odd indeed, for each barb dripped blood — the man could stand no more. While Griselle watched in horror, he picked up the boy and threw him roughly over his knee. Then raising his hand, he prepared to beat the child.

Griselle rushed over to them and thrust her own hand between his and the boy, taking the blow for herself. Then she pulled little Beau to her, crying out, "You are not my husband. He was a gentle man, for all that he went to war. You may have a plume like a flame in your hat, but there is no flame in your heart. The boy is full of mischief, yet still he is the gentler soul." She covered the child's head with kisses. "Go away, and leave me with my boy."

And even though it was Christmas Eve, and even though it broke her heart, she pushed the soldier out the door.

There was little enough for the evening meal, for the soldier had already eaten most of it, but they made the best of what was there. And when it was time for midnight mass at the cathedral, little Beau slipped his hand into Griselle's. As they walked along, he smiled up at her.

When they went through the great cathedral doors, the stone angels inclined their heads downward, whispering to one another like doves cooing: "Such a good woman. Such an ugly child."

This time Griselle heard their voices and looked up at them. "Hush! Tush!" she said. "If a handsome man can be transformed by hate, surely an ugly little boy can be changed by love." She patted Beau on his corn-colored hair. "Can't you see he has grown into his name?" Then she whispered into Beau's ear, "Pay them no mind. They are only stone, after all."

Many years later old Griselle died in her sleep and went straight to heaven. That same night, her ugly son disappeared as well. But if you look very carefully at the angels carved into the facing on the cathedral wall, you will see that not all of them are handsome. There is one with slightly crossed eyes and with teeth almost black. But he is the only one with an absolutely angelic smile.

The illustrations in this book were done in
watercolors on Arches Hot Press Watercolor Paper.
The display type was handlettered by the illustrator.
The text type was set in Cochin
by Thompson Type, San Diego, California.
Color separations were made by Bright Arts, Ltd., Singapore.
Printed and bound by Tien Wah Press, Singapore
Production supervision by Warren Wallerstein and Ginger Boyer
Designed by Lisa Peters

DATE DUE

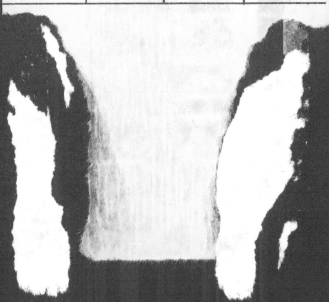